"Little Boy Boo

The Adventures of a Yorkshire terrier
Who Thought He Was a Boy

Written by

David Mercaldo, PhD

Illustrated by

Sophia Silecchia

Write your name here

Copyright©2009 USA by David Mercaldo, Phd

xulon PRESS

Copyright © 2009 by David Mercaldo

Little Boy Boo
by David Mercaldo

Printed in the United States of America

ISBN 978-1-61579-099-9

All rights reserved solely by the author. The author guarantees all contents are original and do not infringe upon the legal rights of any other person or work. No part of this book may be reproduced in any form without the permission of the author. The views expressed in this book are not necessarily those of the publisher.

www.xulonpress.com

Dedicated to Dr. Alan Rubenstein, Veterinarian and all of the children who love and care for their pets

A message from the author...
David Mercaldo

"I'm so glad you have purchased this copy of my book Little Boy Boo. I hope you enjoy reading the adventures as much as I enjoyed writing them. When I thought about illustrating this book I decided to invite <u>you</u> to create your own drawings on the blank page after each chapter. There is even an opportunity to write your own chapter too!"

Use a permanent marker to write your name on the <u>front cover</u>. As the ILLUSTRATOR of this book, you will want to write your own biography on a separate piece of paper and attach it to the <u>rear cover</u> in the space provided.
Attach a <u>picture</u> too.

Little Boy Boo

"Miss Linda's Boy"

The people who lived on Pendale Street knew him as "Miss Linda's Little Boy." Sometimes the children in the neighborhood would come by to play with him, but on most days he would sit on the front porch and watch the world go by.

Of course, he really wasn't a boy. He only thought he was a boy. (Actually...he was a dog!)

If someone asked his owner what kind of dog she was walking, he would growl. He was a little boy and no one was going to call him a dog!

His name was Boo Boo Baxter and he was a Yorkshire terrier. As a puppy he would sneer when people asked his owner, "How old is your Yorkie?" First of all, it was no one's business how old he was and the second thing he would argue is that he wasn't a "Yorkie!" Boo Boo Baxter refused to admit that he was a dog.

The idea of a dog wanting to be a boy all started one afternoon several months after Miss Linda brought him home. On a beautiful June afternoon she took her new puppy for a walk in the park. At the park they saw a lady pushing a baby carriage and heard the cooing of a newborn.

Miss Linda looked in the carriage and smiled as she spoke to the young mother.

"What a charming little boy you have! How adorable...and how bright he looks!"

That did it! Boo Boo liked all of the wonderful things she was saying about the baby and began to jump up and down.

"Oh, do you want to be a little boy too?" she asked him.

Boo Boo kept on jumping and finally let out a happy bark to say, "YES!"

"Okay...from now on you will be my little boy!" Miss Linda promised him.

And that is how a Yorkshire terrier named Boo Boo Baxter became known as..."Miss Linda's Little Boy."

Draw a picture of Boo Boo Baxter

"Boo Boo Baxter's Big Adventure"

If Boo Boo Baxter was really a boy, surely he would do things that little boys do...like getting lost. And one day he did! It happened when he was a little pup.

On a bright spring day Miss Linda opened the back door of the house to let in some fresh air. As a cool breeze came in...a little puppy ran out.

It took only a minute for her to realize he was missing. She called, "BOO BOO!" There was no answer. Miss Linda became very worried, like mothers and fathers do when their little girl or boy is missing.

She ran to the backyard, but he was not there. She looked on one side of the house and then the other. Still there was no Boo Boo. After looking in and out of the house two more times, she ran to her neighbor, Mr. Wilson.

"Did you see him, Mr. Wilson?" Miss Linda cried out as she stepped up to the porch and called to him through the screen door.

"See who!" Mr. Wilson replied.

"My puppy...Boo Boo!" she answered.

"Oh, my....is that little guy lost?" he questioned.

He unlocked the screen door and joined Miss Linda outside. They searched his front and backyard, but there was no sign of the puppy.

Mr. Wilson looked over and saw tears in his neighbor's blue eyes. He also saw a worried look on her face. They were beginning to give up hope when the helpful neighbor spotted Boo Boo.

"There he is!" he cried out.

And there he was...a little black, brown and gold furry mound sat on Mrs. Chan's lawn just a few houses away. He was sitting quietly, watching a bird pull a worm out of the ground. Miss Linda ran over, grabbed Boo Boo up in her arms and began to hug and kiss him.

What she did not know was that Boo Boo ran away when a fat squirrel dug up a nut in her garden and scooted through a hole at the bottom of the fence in the backyard. Somehow Boo Boo managed to squeeze his chubby body through the small opening too.

He never did catch the strange animal but it was indeed Boo Boo's first big adventure.

Draw a picture about this chapter or one of
Miss Linda and Mr. Wilson

"Bee Sting Boo"

Miss Linda enjoyed working in her garden. The neighbors said she had a "green thumb." That meant everything she planted grew tall and beautiful.

Boo Boo remembered the first time he went into the backyard to see his master's beautiful garden.

He stood on the steps of the backyard porch and quietly watched all the things she was doing. As she bent down to work, Boo Boo hopped off the steps and found a comfortable spot on the grass near her. He wanted to learn what "gardening" was all about.

First, Miss Linda took a small shovel and began to dig a hole in the earth. Next, she dropped something in the opening. Then she put the dirt she had removed back into the hole. Finally, the lady gardener sprinkled some water on the spot.

Boo Boo wondered what this was all about because he had never seen Miss Linda do anything like it before.

He looked around the garden. The flowers and plants that were already in bloom were beautiful. It was then that Miss Linda began to hum and in a few minutes her humming turned into singing. Boo Boo listened as she sang a song that explained what she was doing in the garden that day.

"I remember the day when you were a seed
And I put you in the ground
Now I see you're tall and strong with flowers all around!"

That was it! The flowers and plants in the garden came from little seeds.

Boo Boo continued to watch her when all of a sudden, she let out a scream. He had never heard his master scream before and he became frightened. He watched as she grabbed her hand, lifted the garden hose and sprayed water on it. Boo Boo did not understand what was happening to Miss Linda.

"Oh! I've been stung by a bee!" she cried out and continued to spray her hand with the cool water from the hose.

As she spoke, some bees flew down on Boo Boo and stung him on the back and neck. At first it seemed like a little pinch, but then he realized a bee sting could be very painful. He began to feel strange inside and became weak and wobbly.

Miss Linda looked over and saw her little boy stumbling as he tried to walk.

"Oh, no! I think my Little Boy has been stung by a bee too!" she called out.

Miss Linda wasted no time as she lifted Boo Boo into her arms and raced out of the yard and into her car. A few seconds later he was resting on the back seat as the car sped away down the street. But where was Miss Linda going? And how could she drive if she was in pain?

Ten minutes later Boo Boo was lying on an examination table. The sign on the wall read –

DR. ALAN RUBENSTEIN VETERINARIAN

Boo Boo had been to Dr. Rubenstein's office when he was born and then every six months after that for a check-up.

The Doctor examined him then explained to Miss Linda what had happened. "It's a bee sting and you brought him just in time!" Then he turned to the puppy and spoke softly. "This shouldn't hurt too much, Mr. Baxter." (He always called Boo Boo by his last name). He prepared a needle, lifted Boo Boo's fur and gave him a shot.

He spoke in a whisper and gently rubbed his fur. "That didn't hurt too much, did it?"

The doctor looked over and saw Miss Linda rubbing her hand. It was very swollen and red.

"Hey, you were stung too! You're next!" He picked up the phone and made an emergency appointment for her with Dr. Volpe, a people doctor who lived nearby. A few minutes later, Miss Linda was in the doctor's office and she too, received a shot for her bee sting.

The trip home took longer than usual and seemed different to Boo Boo because he couldn't sit up and watch the cars and people on the street. The little pooch was tired and still felt pain from the bee stings.

Soon mother and furry "son" were stepping past the front door of their house on Pendale Street. They were both glad to be home.

Miss Linda tenderly placed her ailing pup in his bed and tip-toed quietly into the kitchen. Surely there would be something tasty waiting for him when she returned, thought Boo Boo. After all, when little boys and little girls are brave, their mothers and fathers always surprise them with a treat!

Draw a picture about this chapter or one of
Boo Boo and Dr. Rubenstein

"A Boy named Frankie"

Miss Linda enjoyed taking walks with Boo Boo and on sunny days you could see them strolling up and down Pendale Street. They would walk up to the end of the block then turn onto Oak Street. Their little trips never took them far from home.

For a little dog there was always something to see or do. For instance, one time Boo Boo saw a strange furry creature crawling on the concrete sidewalk. It must have been the puzzled look on her dog's face that prompted Miss Linda to say something about the little insect he was watching.

"Be gentle Boo!" (Sometimes, she just called him "Boo") "It's a little caterpillar!"

Boo Boo sniffed the inch-long creature and watched as it scrunched its body and stretched it to move forward.

Yes, there was always something interesting going on in the old neighborhood when they took their walks.

In spring or summer the neighborhood was green with life. Hundred year old elm, oak and maple trees towered above the streets. Bushes and foliage wrapped around each house and the air was filled with the sweet smell of flowers.

Sometimes Boo Boo and Miss Linda came upon neighbors who were outside working in their gardens or just sitting on their front porches. When they saw her they would come out to chat and pet Boo Boo. He was a neighborhood favorite.

On a beautiful sunny May morning Miss Linda decided to take a walk with Boo Boo. She strolled up Pendale and then turned on Oak. They would usually stop at that point and turn around, but today she decided to take Boo Boo for a longer walk on Clawson Avenue.

As they turned onto the street they heard loud barking. They both stretched their necks to look through the boxwood hedges to see if it was coming from the red brick house in front of them. Boo Boo found an opening at the bottom of the hedge and Miss Linda peered through an opening at the top. A large white dog came to the hedge and looked through it. Yep! That's where the sound was coming from.

Boo Boo stared in amazement because the dog looked just like him.

He was bigger and all white, but he did look much the same. He was a Highland terrier and weighed about fifteen pounds more than the little Yorkshire terrier standing before him. It was amazing how the two dogs looked so much alike. Then again, they were both terriers and did have many of the same characteristics.

Boo Boo barked to introduce himself and the stranger barked in reply. These were friendly barks...the soft kind that told Miss Linda not to be concerned. The other dog came even closer and squeezed his nose through the leaves to sniff. Boo Boo sniffed back. He had never been nose to nose with another dog before. The sniffing was followed by some more friendly barking.

A moment later a lady came out of the house and called, "Frankie...Oh, Frankie...where are you?" Miss Linda and Boo Boo watched as the dog turned and ran to his owner.

Miss Linda called, "Hello Neighbor!"

The lady came over to the hedge with Frankie nestled in her arms.

"Well, how nice of you to stop and visit," she replied.

"I live over on Pendale, I'm Linda!"

The neighbor lady smiled and introduced herself. Miss Linda picked up Boo Boo and the two dogs stared quietly at each other. When they both began to squeal, their owners put them back down on the ground and once again they scurried to find the opening at the bottom of the hedge. When they finally reached the opening the terriers began to sniff each other's nose once again.

The lady invited Miss Linda into her yard to see her garden.

"He usually barks when dogs walk by our house, but he sure does like your little dog!" she said as they walked around the garden admiring the flowers.

"I think our terriers are going to get along just fine," Miss Linda added as she reached down to lovingly pat Boo Boo.

"I'm so glad too! Frankie gets awfully lonely behind this big hedge," said the neighbor. Then turning to her dog Frankie she said, "How would you like to have your new friend, Boo Boo, come and visit us from time to time?" Frankie let out a happy bark and so did Boo Boo.

The women smiled at each other and wondered if the dogs really understood what they were saying. (Of course, children know that they do).

"It sure looks like we're going to be good neighbors!" said Miss Linda.

So that was the beginning of a wonderful friendship for the ladies who lived on Pendale and Clawson...and their "boys" of course!

Draw a picture about this chapter or one of
Boo Boo and Frankie

"Boo Boo Baxter to the Rescue"

If ever there was a quiet dog, Boo Boo Baxter was one! He rarely barked and often went for days on end without making a sound. Miss Linda and he had a special kind of language. They seemed to know what each was thinking. It was a wonderful relationship, and in Boo Boo's case barking was not necessary. She just knew what he wanted or needed!

On the rare occasion when he did "speak," Miss Linda understood what he wanted, like the time he was locked in the cellar by accident and whimpered for help. It was a different kind of "call" and Miss Linda knew exactly what he wanted and freed him from the basement.

Boo Boo Baxter led a simple life. During the day he would sit by Miss Linda's rocking chair and at night he slept on the floor at the foot of her bed...that is when he wasn't in the kitchen having a late night snack. Yes, life was quiet and peaceful in their house on Pendale Street.

However, there was one time that he had to bark as loud as he could.

It happened one Christmas Eve when all of the houses on the street were ablaze with holiday lights of green, red, blue, yellow, orange and purple. The old grandfather clock in the hallway chimed and the whistling bird came out of a little door to chirp that it was 1:30 am. Other than this little sound, the house was quiet and Miss Linda was fast asleep in her bed under a warm quilt.

She usually slept with the window slightly opened at the bottom to let a little of the cool night air into the room. But something was different about the air that night. It had an unusual odor.

The little watchdog stretched his body as high as it could go and stared out of the window into the night. He looked across the street and to his surprise he saw flames coming from a neighbor's home.

Boo Boo ran to Miss Linda's bed and began to bark. At first it was a soft bark, but when he saw that his master didn't wake up, he began to run around the room barking and jumping. He had never done this before.

Startled by her dog's barking and jumping, Miss Linda rose and followed him to the window. Sure enough the big corner house was on fire. She ran to the phone and dialed 911; then she called her neighbors to see if they were still sleeping.

As you might expect they were all fast asleep in their beds. Her phone call awakened them. The entire family left the house at Miss Linda's warning and ran into the street to safety.

Within minutes the night air was filled with smoke and the sound of sirens. Two fire trucks raced around the corner and in minutes the fire was being drenched with powerful streams of water.

It took the firemen two hours to put the fire completely out.

Later, Miss Linda and some of the other neighbors were gathered in her living room eating some snacks she had quickly prepared. Boo Boo knew all about Miss Linda's snacks. They were always delicious! The neighbors thought so too!

The neighbor, whose house caught on fire, walked over and thanked Miss Linda for saving her family and home.

"If it wasn't for you we might have been killed!" she said.

She put her arms around Miss Linda and began to cry. Miss Linda looked across the room and saw Boo Boo playing with some of the other neighbors. If he had not awakened her from a deep sleep, the entire family might have been seriously injured or even killed by the fire.

"Dear neighbor, I think we have to thank a little boy named, Boo Boo Baxter for saving your family," offered Miss Linda. The thankful neighbor looked over at the little Yorkshire terrier and sobbed. Then she told Miss Linda, "You have such a wonderful little boy!"

It was almost daybreak when the little furry hero finally lay in his bed sleeping. Miss Linda leaned down and kissed him on the head.

"You've been a busy little boy today!"

The weary little pooch could barely open his eyes as he listened to Miss Linda's words. It had been an incredible night for all of the neighbors and an amazing dog...named Boo Boo Baxter.

Draw a picture about this chapter or one of
Boo Boo at the bed barking to wake Miss Linda

"Belly Boo"

Thanksgiving was always a special day at Miss Linda's house. Her family and friends gathered to give thanks for all the things that had happened to them during the year since they last met. Aunt Matilda from Vermont and "Good Ole" Mr. Wilson were there too!

Someone else always came to the annual feast...Aunt Matilda's dog, Simon. He was an irritable and stubborn black Pug. Most of the time he just slept at his owner's feet, but he was bossy and sometimes got on Boo Boo's nerves. That's when they would bark and growl at each other. Since it was only once a year, Boo Boo decided he could put up with the fussing and fighting and tried to be as friendly as possible.

This year the guests arrived around noon. One by one they gathered in front of the fireplace and talked about the good old times and the new times too! The two dogs sat near the warm, glowing flames. Simon seemed to be in a quiet mood this year and Boo Boo was glad for that.

At three o'clock the hostess brought out a big turkey with all the necessary trimmings.

When everyone was seated at the dining room table, Miss Linda asked Mr. Wilson to pray a blessing on the food. As usual, it was a very long prayer and when he finally said, "amen," Boo Boo let out a happy bark and everyone began to laugh.

He took his place at Miss Linda's feet as she began to carve the big bird. Occasionally, a piece of turkey or some gravy dropped, but most of the time it didn't reach the floor before Boo Boo gobbled it up. There was some competition from Simon, but there was always enough for both of them.

There seemed to be more scraps on the floor under the table than in years past. The Yorkie and Pug moved from foot to foot, finding pieces of sweet potato, stuffing, turkey meat and of course Boo Boo's favorite treat, cranberries. While the folks ate a feast on the table, the dogs ate one under it.

During the meal there was some growling under the table, but the two dogs seemed satisfied with the scraps they found there.

Throughout the day Boo Boo ran around the house, performed tricks and ate more food than he had ever eaten before. Wherever people were eating, Boo Boo was there. In the living room he caught and gobbled a piece of carrot cake midair that Mr. Wilson dropped while bending down to sit on Miss Linda's rocker. Aunt Matilda also contributed some crunchy gingersnap cookies when she dropped her dish on the hallway rug.

Boo Boo Baxter didn't know how much food would fit in his little tummy, but he was willing to find out! Simon took on the challenge too!

The children also left all kinds of "goodies" on tables, chairs and the floor. It was a feast for Boo Boo and he hoped it would never end. He thought it was the best Thanksgiving ever! The look on Simon's face showed that he felt the same way too! In the late afternoon both dogs rested at the feet of their master.

At around 7:00 pm the guests began to leave and Miss Linda started to clean up. She was a hard worker and Boo Boo watched as she vacuumed, washed and dusted. She would not have to work as hard this year because he had already eaten most of the bits and pieces of food that had fallen on the floor throughout the day.

When 9:00 o'clock arrived, Miss Linda sat down on her rocker and began to doze. That was not the case with Boo Boo Baxter. Something was wrong! Deep inside his little tummy he could feel something churning. A painful expression on his face replaced the happy look he had a few hours before.

Finally, he barked and woke Miss Linda from her slumber. She looked down at Boo Boo and knew immediately that something was wrong. He was sick! As she went to pet him, he moaned and could not move his little body to meet her hand. She wanted to pick him up but he was too sick to move and cried out in pain when she tried to touch his swollen belly.

"Little boy," she called to him, "I think you ate tooooo much today and now you are ill."

The little canine lay on the floor motionless. Miss Linda called to him, "I know what you need...and I'm going to fix you up!"

Boo Boo gave out a hopeful whine and stared as Miss Linda disappeared into the kitchen. Before long she returned with a little bowl in her hand. She placed it by Boo Boo's mouth, but he didn't have the strength to reach it. Gently, she lifted his head and watched as his tongue lapped up some of the special broth she had prepared.

There must be some medicine in it, Boo Boo thought, because in a few minutes his stomach began to feel all bubbly and tingly. Then he let out a big belch. It was the biggest belch he had ever heard. It startled him and Miss Linda chuckled when she heard it. "I think you'll feel a lot better now, my little boy!"

Later, she carried Boo Boo to his cuddle bed at the foot of her own bed. Miss Linda got down on the floor and scooted close to him. Then she sang a sweet song:

"Little boy you're tired
And little boy you're blue
Little boy you've had a busy day."

When she finished singing, Miss Linda blew a kiss to him. A little whimper could be heard as if Boo Boo was trying to say, "Thanks Mom!'

Yes, Miss Linda's little boy had a VERY busy day.

Draw a picture about this chapter or one of
Boo Boo and Simon sitting under the table

"Boo Boo Baxter meets Mr. Snowman"

There were many people who enjoyed visiting Miss Linda and Boo Boo.

The mailman came everyday except Sunday.

Mr. Gill, the neighbor from down the street, showed up once a week to bring his homemade cookies. Boo Boo thought they tasted terrible but he always ate one so Mr. Gill wouldn't feel bad. Usually, he would stay for lunch and sometimes, if he got to talking, he'd hang around for dinner too!

And then there was George the repairman. He'd show up at the front door with his box of tools. The neighbors said he could fix anything and they were right! When he did come to the house, he would usually find something to repair or paint. He never charged Miss Linda for any of his work, but gladly accepted her invitations to stay for breakfast or lunch or dinner.

Sometimes the mailman, Mr. Gill, George and Mr. Wilson, their neighbor, would arrive on the same day and at the same time! Miss Linda didn't mind because she figured it was a great opportunity to try out a new recipe...or two!

But a new visitor arrived one day in February when it began to snow.

Boo Boo and Miss Linda were getting ready to go to sleep. Before turning out the lights, she called him over to look out of the window. He stared out into the night and seemed puzzled by the snow-filled air that he was seeing for the first time. Miss Linda smiled and explained.

"In the morning everything will be covered in white. You've never seen snow before and I think you're going to enjoy it."

That night the little pup fell into a deep sleep. When morning arrived he didn't hear Miss Linda leave from the front door to clean the snow in the front walkway. It was the shovel scraping over the stones that finally woke the sleepy little dog. He walked slowly down the stairs and looked out of the glass of the front storm door.

Before him was a snow-covered world he had never seen before.

He saw Miss Linda clearing the snow from the walkway and he saw something else. A stranger was sitting in the front yard. He was made of three balls of snow: a large one to hold him up, a medium-sized one for a body and a small one for a head. He had two rocks for eyes, tree branches for arms, a long carrot for a nose and a mouth carved in the shape of a half moon with acorns for teeth. On top of his head was a big black top hat.

Boo Boo studied the new arrival and let out a quiet bark to see if he would move, but he didn't. Even when the wind blew snow dust on him, he still didn't move.

He was staring at the visitor and watched as Miss Linda walked over, kneeled down and gently patted him on the tummy.

"Hello, Mr. Snowman!" she said.

So that's what this was all about! A man made out of snow! Of course it wasn't a real man...just something made from the snow by Miss Linda.

When she finished cleaning a path all around the house, she climbed up the two porch steps and opened the door. Seeing this, Boo Boo bounded out and ran to

"Mr. Snowman." He looked up at his smiling face and jumped up to inspect him.

Yep! He was a snowman all right! Boo Boo let out a kind bark to welcome him. "He'll be around for a few days, Boo. You take good care of him, okay?" Miss Linda spoke.

Boo Boo Baxter walked to the top step of the porch and looked over his front yard and his little world. It wasn't a big world, like where city dogs lived. It didn't have busy streets or parks where dogs met and played together. No, Boo Boo's world was quiet and today a stranger would join him and share it.

He really didn't know how many days Mr. Snowman would be visiting, but no matter how long, Boo Boo would protect him until it was time for him to leave and go home to his world and his house.

The little guard dog went out every day to visit the snowman, and as the days passed, something extraordinary was happening to his visitor. He was getting smaller and smaller and soon he was Boo Boo's size.

Then one day he heard the sound of rain tapping on the front window. Through the drizzle he saw that Mr.

Snowman was gone. When the rain finally stopped, Miss Linda opened the front door and Boo Boo darted out to the place where the visitor had once stood. While he was busy sniffing the ground, Miss Linda came over and kneeled down just like she had done the day the Snowman first appeared. She lifted Boo Boo into her arms and spoke.

"Little boy...don't be sad! Mr. Snowman will come back to our front yard some day."

Miss Linda's little boy didn't know how or when the man made of snow would return. But sometimes, when he felt lonely, he would gaze out of the window at the place where the snowman had once stood. He'd stare into the sky and wonder where the visitor had gone. The little Yorkshire terrier knew he could believe his owner who promised that someday Mr. Snowman would return. And when he did, Boo Boo Baxter would welcome him into his yard and his little world.

Draw a picture about this chapter or one of
Boo Boo and the Snowman

"The New Boy on the Block"

Pendale was an old street with old houses and people who had lived there for many years. Boo Boo couldn't remember when a new family moved into the neighborhood. Everything was as it had been for a long, long time. The trees grew taller, the bushes fuller and the tulips more colorful. Yes, things didn't change much on Pendale Street.

Of course some things don't last forever, and on a chilly day in January a new family moved into the old run-down house at the end of the street. No one had lived in it for many years and Boo Boo couldn't imagine who would want to live there. But on that day a moving van arrived early in the morning and two men began to unload boxes, furniture and toys. On the lawn were bicycles, wagons and other kinds of things that assured Boo Boo some of his new neighbors were children.

In the late afternoon a car pulled up to the house and Miss Linda and Boo Boo watched as the family stepped out.

There was a man and a woman, a little girl and a boy. Boo Boo knew that Miss Linda would go over and greet their new neighbors and sure enough, a few days later, the two made their way down the street to the house. With one hand Miss Linda held Boo Boo's leash and in the other a fresh apple pie.

As they came close to the house they saw painters giving it a fresh coat of white paint.

Miss Linda knocked on the front door and Boo Boo lifted his paws and scratched at the bottom. A woman opened it and introduced herself. Soon after, Boo Boo was sitting on his owner's lap in the living room. Boxes were everywhere and so was the scent of hot apple pie! The lady brought two cups of tea and the neighbors began to chat. Boo Boo looked around and saw toys scattered everywhere.

He was about to doze when the little girl entered the room. "Oh, look at the puppy!" she cried out happily.

The youngster walked slowly over to Boo Boo and began to pet him. Her hand was soft and she was a gentle patter. Boo Boo liked gentle "patters."

46

"My daughter, Christie, loves animals!" the lady said.

"Would you like to hold him?" Miss Linda asked.

"Oh yes! May I, Mommy?" she asked her mother.

Miss Linda carefully placed Boo Boo into the arms of Christie.

As he was getting comfortable and ready to close his eyes, the little girl's brother arrived panting and all out of breath.

When he saw his sister holding Boo Boo, he ran over and grabbed him out of her lap. He was lifting him into the air when Miss Linda begged him. "Please be gentle with Boo Boo!" Boo Boo Baxter growled because he wasn't the least bit happy with what the boy was doing.

"Boo Boo? Hah! What a stupid name!" the boy called out.

"Please!" Miss Linda repeated.

"AW! He's just a dog. I don't have to be gentle!" he replied.

47

"Randall, you listen to the lady!" his mother demanded.

He released Boo Boo into his sister's arms and asked, "What's for lunch?"

Miss Linda stood up and thanked her new neighbor for the tea. Then she turned and walked to the door.

"Oh, it was my pleasure and it was very thoughtful of you to bring a pie!" the lady replied adding, "Please stop by again!" The women exchanged phone numbers and promised to meet again soon.

Boo Boo thought to himself that he wouldn't want to return if it meant getting harsh treatment from Randall, who thought he was "just a dog."

A winter storm came two weeks later and brought more than a foot of snow to the neighborhood. Boo Boo loved the snow and begged to go out in the front yard to play. Miss Linda bundled him up in his little red sweater, then opened the front door and watched as he ran out into the mounds of snow that covered the front yard.

It wasn't long before a few of the neighborhood kids came out to play in the snow. Boo Boo was busy exploring his front yard, sniffing the snow and looking at things the wind had blown into his little world. He was playing quietly when all of a sudden he felt the crushing blow of a hard-packed snowball as it hit his furry little body and splattered apart. It hurt! Oh, it hurt worse than anything that ever happened to him.

Boo Boo looked up and saw his new neighbor, Randall. He was laughing as he stood in the street and called to him. "Gottcha!"

The injured dog barked to let the boy know he was in pain and very mad. How could anyone do this to him?

The boy ran away and Boo Boo fell to the ground to rest his hurting body.

A little while later, the street was full of children playing in the snow. The big boys were throwing snowballs at one of the kids. Boo Boo looked up and saw that Randall was their target. He was crying as the boys chased him up and down the street. He ran as fast as he could, but no matter how fast he ran, the snowballs continued to strike him.

Finally, he opened up Boo Boo's front gate and fell to the ground. The big boys were right behind, standing outside of the fence with snowballs in their hands.

The little dog knew that something must be done to help his young neighbor. He barked and snarled enough to scare anyone! The boys knew that Boo Boo was mad and didn't stick around to see what he might do to them. They stopped throwing snowballs and ran down the street.

Boo Boo and Randall were now alone and something wonderful happened. The little dog ambled over to him and began to lick the salty tears from his face. The boy reached over and pulled him to his side.

"Thanks boy!" he said.

Boo Boo looked at him and then snuggled even closer to try and comfort him.

"Thanks for saving me...I'll never forget what you did for me today!" he finished. Then he kissed his little four-legged friend on the head.

Miss Linda opened the front door and called, "Boo Boo, it's time to come in now!"

"Hi Miss," the boy called.

"How are you today, Randall?" she asked.

"I'm fine now...because your dog saved me," he answered.

"Well, why don't you both come in and have some soup! It looks like a soup day if you ask me...and there is plenty for everyone! I'll call your mom and let her know that you are here," Miss Linda said as she opened the door for the *two* boys!

Boo Boo could not believe that this was the same boy who had grabbed him when they first met.

Miss Linda watched and smiled as the big pot of soup went from full to empty.

"Can I come back and play with your dog?" Randall asked.

"Well, I always let Boo Boo decide those kinds of things! What do you think, Boo?" she asked

He walked to the boy and offered him his right paw. Miss Linda smiled, "You are always welcome here anytime you would like to come!"

A moment later Boo Boo watched from the front doorway as Randall made his way through the yard and out into the deep snow that covered the street. The grateful neighbor turned and called, "Thank you, Boo Boy!" (No one had ever called him "Boo Boy!")

As Randall walked down the street to his house, Miss Linda reached over to pet her little hero and spoke gently to him. "Boo Boo Baxter you're quite a brave little boy...and I think you have made a new friend, don't you?"

Then she lifted him gently, smiled and hugged him.

"I love you little boy!" she told him.

Boo Boo Baxter knew those words. He had heard them many, many times before and responded with a little bark, as if to say, "I love you too, Mom!"

Draw a picture about this chapter or one of
Boo Boo and his neighbor Randall

"The Day Mimi Came to Town"

Miss Linda loved to have guests in her home! In summer, winter, spring or fall, family members and friends would sit around the big dining room table and talk for hours about everything and anything. Boo Boo would sit under the table and listen. Sometimes, he would fall into a deep sleep, only to be awakened by laughter or a slight kick when someone got up or shifted.

Miss Linda spent many hours preparing her favorite dishes for these visits and Boo Boo Baxter never left the kitchen when she was cooking. The sweet aroma of her baking or the robust scent of steak sizzling in the broiler, were all familiar to a dog whose favorite activity was eating.

Sometimes, Miss Linda would try to fool him. She would pick up some morsels of his dog food and hold them to her lips. Then she would say, "Yummy, Yummy!" Boo Boo was fooled only once by this little 'trick' and he was amazed that she tried it over and over again. Anyway, it was just a game she played with him from time to time.

One day, Miss Linda invited an old friend from elementary school to come for lunch. Boo Boo thought the table she had set looked beautiful. It had a white table cloth with pink napkins and placemats. There were silver spoons lying next to cream colored dishes and a vase filled with fresh flowers in the middle of the table.

In the kitchen, Boo Boo stretched his little body as far as he could and sniffed the piping hot peach pie that was cooling on the top of the stove.

A moment later, he left the kitchen, walked over to the table and slumped down. It was time for his nap, but just as he closed his eyes the doorbell rang. Boo Boo watched as a big smile came over the face of his master.

"Karen, welcome to my home!" Miss Linda called out as she embraced her friend from so many years ago.

"Linda, you haven't change a bit. You're just as beautiful as you were when we were little girls in kindergarten!" the visitor responded. Of course, Boo Boo Baxter thought he had the most beautiful owner in the whole wide world.

He listened to the old friends talk for a few minutes and as they were about to enter the dining room, he heard a bark. It was a little bark; the kind that a puppy makes. He looked across the room and saw a little dog peering through the glass of the front storm door.

"Oh, you brought your puppy!" said Miss Linda.

"Mimi can wait on the porch. She'll be fine there!" Karen replied.

"Nonsense...she can come right in and join us! Right, Boo Boo?" she said as she pushed the door open to let the little pooch into the room.

The stranger bounded into the house and ran straight at Boo Boo. At first there was staring, some sniffing and then a whole lot of barking. The little pup began to jump on Boo Boo and that made him very mad. He snapped back with an angry bark and thought; *Why did Miss Linda let this menace into my house?*

"Oh, how cute she is!" declared Miss Linda as she pulled the puppy close and rubbed noses with her.

"Let's have some pie!" she continued.

A few minutes later the childhood girlfriends sat across from each other laughing and joking about the past. Nestled in Miss Linda's arms was the puppy.

"When and how did you get Mimi?" she asked curiously.

"I found her while traveling on my way to visit some friends. I stopped at a farm to ask for directions. Posted on the front door was a sign that read, *FRENCH POODLE PUPPIES FOR SALE*. Well...I knocked on the door and the farmer's wife gave me directions. I then asked her about the puppies and she said there was just one left. We walked to the barn and there in a little wooden pen was one lonely female puppy. I fell in love the moment I saw her. That was four months ago. She's such an angel!"

When the ladies finished their pie, Miss Linda gently laid Mimi down in front of Boo Boo. Thinking the little dog had quieted down, Boo Boo let down his guard, but the puppy again jumped on him again and pawed his face. Boo Boo was angry with her.

"*ENOUGH IS ENOUGH*!" he growled. Hearing this, Miss Linda started to scold him.

"Now you stop that, BAXTER!" she cried out. (She only called him "Baxter" when she was angry with the way he was behaving).

Boo Boo Baxter, MASTER OF THE HOUSE, could not believe her words. What was he supposed to stop? This dog was making all of the trouble. Then things got worse!

The little pup ran into the kitchen and drank from Boo Boo's water dish. "Oh, how cute!" said Miss Linda. Boo Boo growled quietly to himself.

Then Mimi ran to Boo Boo's bowl of food and gulped down some of his favorite chow. "Isn't she something else?" Miss Linda continued.

Boo Boo growled again, but this time a little louder.

In a flash Mimi ran to Boo Boo's living room and plopped down in his cuddle bed, acting like she owned it.

Boo Boo growled and barked so loud the whole the whole neighborhood could hear him.

Then the little poodle got up and ran around looking for something else to do. And she found it! Mimi spotted one of Boo Boo's toys lying on a chair.

Seeing that it was out of reach, she hopped up on the chair next to it, which was a little lower. Then she jumped from chair to chair, finally reaching the toy.

"My goodness! What a resourceful puppy you have, Karen!" Miss Linda stated.

That did it! First, Mimi drank his water, then she ate his food. Next, she messed up his cuddle bed and now bit into his favorite toy. Boo Boo ran to Mimi and yanked the toy right out of her mouth. No one was going to play with his toy...his favorite toy.

Miss Linda stood up and demanded that he give his toy to the guest. Boo Boo released it from his mouth and let it drop to the floor. When he did, Miss Linda pointed her finger at him and scolded him, demanding, "This is our guest and you have to share, Baxter!"

Boo Boo figured there was nothing else he could do because Miss Linda was giving Mimi the run of the house. And run she did! The puppy was full of energy and wouldn't sit still. Boo Boo hoped the visit wouldn't last too long.

Finally, an hour later, Miss Karen announced that she had to leave.

Boo Boo was relieved. At last he could have his house back again. After all it was *his house*!

When Miss Linda had cleared the dishes and put away the remainder of the pie, she sat down on her favorite chair and turned on the radio. Boo Boo found a comfortable spot in his cuddle bed. The tired host tuned the radio to a station that played her favorite kind of music... opera. Boo Boo loved opera music too!

As the music was playing, Miss Linda lowered the volume on the radio, looked down and smiled at Boo Boo. "Mimi is so cute. Why didn't you like her, Boo?"

He didn't bark a reply. He was angry at Mimi. How dare she do all these terrible things during her visit to his house?

"She's so full of energy...just like you were when you were a little puppy. Do remember Boo?" Miss Linda continued.

Boo Boo Baxter was silent. He was angry! No, he was very angry!

"Yes, you were just like little Mimi when I brought you home! Don't you remember when we visited Mrs. Goodwin, down the street? You did the same things to her dog that Mimi did to you. I remember how her big Boxer, Max, barked and made such a fuss when you ate from his food dish, drank from his bowl, jumped in his bed...and even ran around the house playing with his favorite toy. Max has not forgotten your first visit and still barks at you when we walk by his house."

Boo Boo sat quietly and listened. Did he do all those things when he was a puppy?

"Yes, you were quite an active puppy, you were!" Miss Linda reminded him.

So he used to be just like Mimi! As he thought about his "puppy days," he decided to forgive her for doing things puppies do! After all, he was a puppy once too!

Then came some surprising news!

"Oh, I forgot to tell you...Karen is planning to spend a weekend with us next summer. Maybe we'll rent a cottage down on the beach. You and Mimi will have a wonderful time together!" Miss Linda announced.

Oh, no! A whole weekend with Mimi! Boo Boo worried.

"She'll be a big dog then and you two will get along just fine!" Miss Linda promised.

Boo Boo Baxter let out a little bark. It was the kind that let Miss Linda know everything would be just fine next summer...that is as long as Mimi would no longer be a puppy.

Draw a picture about this chapter or one of
Boo Boo, Mimi, Miss Linda and Karen.

"Teddy Bear Boo"

For Boo Boo Baxter, there was nothing he enjoyed more than a walk in the park. Whenever Miss Linda said the word "park," he would jump up and down and run to the front door. You might think most people enjoy going to a park on a bright sunny day, but that was not Boo Boo's favorite time to go there. He loved the winter months when the air was chilly. Miss Linda would bundle him up in his favorite red sweater and off they would go to the park.

On a wintry day she looked down at her boy Boo Boo and smiled. "I bet you could use some fresh air! Would you like to go to the park?" she asked. (Boo Boo had been in the house for a whole week).

The happy pooch jumped into Miss Linda's arms and licked her nose.

She slipped into a long coat, wrapped a scarf around her neck and put on her warmest woolen mittens. She bundled Boo Boo too...in his red sweater. In the twinkling of an eye they were on their way to the park. As they crossed the street a snowflake landed on Boo Boo's nose. A few feet later he felt more snowflakes. By the time they neared the park it was snowing lightly. Oh how Boo Boo Baxter loved to run in the snow!

When they arrived at the park they saw children playing and Miss Linda let Boo Boo join them. They all knew their favorite Yorkshire terrier and right away started to play a game of "fetch the stick" with him.

While he played, Miss Linda took a seat on one of the park benches where a lady was sitting with a little girl. The two women talked for a few minutes and Miss Linda learned that the lady's name was Annie and the little girl's name was Amy.

"She'll be three years old on Saturday and I have planned a big party for her!" Annie announced.

"Well, I've got a birthday boy in my house and he'll be six years old next week!" Miss Linda replied.

"You have a boy?" questioned Annie.

"Not really. Boo Boo, my little Yorkshire terrier thinks he's a boy!" (Miss Linda whispered so Boo Boo, who was playing nearby, wouldn't hear her).

The small dog was having a wonderful time playing with the children, but after fifteen minutes of running and chasing after the stick he grew tired and came to Miss Linda's side to rest. She reached down and lifted him onto the bench.

The little girl Amy came over to pet Boo Boo. He was glad to have someone move the wet snow off of his fur. She had gentle hands and knew just the right way to stroke his fur. He snuggled close to her and as he did, the snow began to fall from the sky like big cotton balls.

The young mother stood up and announced that she had to hurry home to prepare dinner for her family. Boo Boo was very sorry to see the little girl go. He looked up at her and she leaned down to kiss him on the head as the ladies were busy exchanging phone numbers and house addresses.

"Isn't she a little princess!" commented Miss Linda as she waved goodbye to mother and daughter. Boo Boo couldn't agree more. That little princess could pet him whenever she wanted, he thought.

Boo Boo Baxter wondered if he would ever see the little girl again and became sad when he thought that maybe he wouldn't.

At that same moment they saw their neighbor, Mr. Wilson. He was enjoying the park too! Boo Boo jumped off the bench to greet him. But he was distracted. To his surprise, when he reached the snowy ground, he saw a little stuffed toy bear lying on the snow under the bench. He stopped to sniff the teddy bear and knew immediately to whom it belonged.

Mr. Wilson came over to say hello, then turned and started to walk home. But all the time, the little dog could not take his eyes from the stuffed animal.

Boo Boo decided to take the bear home and hoped that someday he might be able to return it to its owner.

The snow began to really come down fast and hard, so Miss Linda decided to put his leash on. When she was finished he leaned over and quickly snatched the bear between his teeth.

The two headed on home and into the blinding snow. Miss Linda was hoping to arrive before they couldn't see at all. On the way home Boo Boo followed behind so she didn't see what he was carrying in his mouth.

But when Miss Linda opened the front door she did see the stuffed teddy bear and reached for it. But Boo Boo wouldn't let it go.

"This belongs to someone and you took it...bad boy!" she started. "Where and when did you get this, Baxter?" she sternly questioned him.

Boo Boo ran to his bed and brought the toy along. Miss Linda was puzzled because he had never done anything like this before.

"I can't imagine why you want a silly teddy bear anyway. You have plenty of toys!" Linda called to him.

Several times during the evening she tried to take the bear from Boo Boo, but he wouldn't let it go.

"Baxter...I don't know what has come over you, but I'm going to bed. In the morning we'll settle this matter!" she said as she turned out the light.

That night Boo Boo slept with the stuffed toy bear next to him. No one was going to take this bear from him but its real owner.

When morning arrived Boo Boo was sitting in his bed with the teddy bear hanging from his mouth. He looked adorable, thought Miss Linda. After stretching and yawning, she looked outside and saw the new fallen snow. It must be ten inches deep, she figured.

"Well...here we go again! I'll get the shovel and you can watch from the window as I clean the walkway," she told Boo. She dressed quickly, put on her warmest coat and mittens, and then left from the front door.

When she turned around, there he was...looking out of the window with the bear clenched between his teeth.

It was almost an hour later when she went back into the house and set a fresh pot of tea on the table. She looked over at Boo Boo and saw a hungry look on his face.

"Hey, little fella, I didn't feed you yet...shame on me!" she apologized.

She placed Boo Boo's feeding dish on the floor but he wouldn't let go of the teddy bear long enough to take even one bite.

Miss Linda didn't know what to think. What was this teddy bear business all about?

As she was about to take a bite of her muffin, there was a knock on the door. It was Annie and her little girl, Amy.

All of sudden Boo Boo started jumping up on Miss Linda and called out a happy bark.

"Hello, Annie!" Miss Linda said as she opened the door.

"Good morning, Linda. I am on a treasure hunt. I do hope you can help me," Annie said.

"Treasure hunt?" questioned Miss Linda

"Amy lost her teddy bear and cried all night long. I thought maybe you or Boo Boo saw it," Annie answered.

"Saw it? I've been living with it since we arrived home yesterday from the park," Miss Linda replied.

The women noticed that Boo Boo had already brought the stuffed toy to Amy, who was hugging and kissing it.

"So that's what this is all about!" called Miss Linda.

"Thank you, Boo Boo!" Annie said as she kneeled down to pet him.

"Boo Boo Baxter made it his personal duty to hold on to this bear and protect it!" Miss Linda said as she petted him.

"Well, I'm sure glad he did," Annie agreed.

A few minutes later the ladies were enjoying some of Miss Linda's tea and muffins. Nearby, a little girl, a teddy bear and a happy pooch sat playing. It certainly was a wonderful day for everyone...especially for a little boy named BOO BOO.

Draw a picture about this chapter or one of
Boo Boo holding the teddy bear in his mouth

"Sailor Boy Boo"

Miss Linda and Boo Boo Baxter lived in New York City on Staten Island. The ocean was only a half-mile from their house and they went there often to sit and watch the birds and boats. They both loved the smell of the salty sea air and the little restaurant where they occasionally ate lunch or dinner. It had an outdoor patio where pets were allowed to sit at the feet of their owners.

Miss Linda usually ordered a little hamburger for Boo Boo and gave him some of her fries as a treat. During the cool fall months when the restaurant was still open, she would order hot soup...a small bowl for Boo Boo and a big one for herself.

When they finished they would sit and bask in the cool sea air.

Now it happened one particular day that a friend joined Miss Linda for lunch. As they talked, Boo Boo found a comfortable spot under the table and began to doze. The noise from the seagulls and boat motors roused him and he decided to take a walk on the boat pier. The little "sea lover" was always careful not to get too close to the edge because he was afraid that he might fall into the water. Soon he was all the way down at the end of the pier, much farther than he had ever gone before. He felt safe because he could still look back and see Miss Linda in the distance talking to her friend.

As he stood there he raised his head and nose into the air and smelled something. He thought it might be a steak sizzling on a barbecue. His curiosity took him over to a boat where a man was cooking. It was steak all right!

"Come on over, boy!" called a friendly voice.

Boo Boo wandered over to the man and wondered if he might be getting a piece of that steak. He moved cautiously closer to the boat and opened his mouth wide as the man tossed a piece of beef into the air. He caught it before it hit the ground. The steak tasted delicious and the man offered him some more.

"Come on boy, come on board!" the man invited.

It was too tempting to resist, so Boo Boo Baxter leaped on board the big boat. He chomped on a few more pieces of the delicious beef. When his belly was full he became sleepy, so he decided to take a nap. He didn't know how long he slept, but when he opened his eyes he saw that sky was darkening. He knew it was getting late and decided to walk back to Miss Linda.

The man saw that he wanted to leave, so he pet Boo Boo and said "goodbye, boy!" Then he turned to clean the barbecue.

What happened next was not to be expected! Boo Boo began to climb over some empty boxes and fell into one. The cover came crashing down on him. The man did not notice what happened and a few minutes later left his boat and walked off the dock. Boo Boo Baxter was now on board a boat, trapped inside a wooden box and hidden from everyone.

He began to bark, but no one heard him. He tried to bark louder, but still no one heard him.

Miss Linda had been calling for him but Boo Boo could not hear her. She searched the dockside for over an hour. She was worried and wondered if he had left the dock and was walking somewhere on the shoreline. She called the police and asked if anyone had found a stray dog. The policeman on the phone said, "Nope...no lost dogs reported here!"

Her dog was missing and she didn't know what else to do! Two hours later she was still searching the shoreline, boats and anywhere he might have gone in the area. She began to think that Boo Boo Baxter was lost...forever! Tears filled her eyes as she sat in her car all alone, ready to drive home to an empty house.

"May I help you, lady?" a man's voice called. Miss Linda looked out of the window to see a man carrying a fishing pole and an ice chest.

"My little dog is missing and I don't know what to do!" she told him.

"Can you tell me what he looks like...I mean the color and kind of dog?" he asked.

"He's...he's..." Miss Linda could not finish her reply because tears began to flow from her eyes.

"He's a Yorkshire terrier. Two years old...and..." she said with a tearful voice.

"A Yorkie, you say? One came on my boat in the late afternoon and ate half of my steak. He did leave when...

WAIT A MINUTE…maybe he didn't leave. I never really saw him get off the boat. Why don't you come with me and we'll take a look before I pull out to do some night fishing!"

Miss Linda and the man walked down the dock to his boat. As they approached it, Miss Linda stopped and listened.

"Do you hear that?"

"Hear what?" the man answered.

"Listen…do you hear a dog barking?" She asked.

A few steps later they were on board the craft, but there was no sign of Boo Boo. Where was he? Then the faint sound of a dog yelping was heard again.

"That's my Boo! He's got to be somewhere on this boat." Miss Linda said as the man went down into the cabin to check if he was there.

"Well, he's not down there!" he said as he climbed the steps to the main deck a few seconds later.

"Listen!" Miss Linda said again.

"I hear it too!" the man said as he walked to the empty boxes lying on board deck. He thought they were empty, but decided to open them anyway. He lifted one of the covers, but there was no Boo Boo. He lifted another. Still, there was no Boo Boo. By now Miss Linda joined him in checking the boxes and sure enough, as she lifted the lid of the last one... a tired, sweaty and smelly little dog cried out.

"My boy!" Miss Linda excitedly called out as she lifted the little dog from the box. Boo Boo Baxter was exhausted. Nothing like this had ever happened to him.

"Well I'll be a shipwrecked skipper if that ain't the strangest thing that ever happened aboard this boat!" the man declared.

Miss Linda carried Boo Boo all the way to her car and drove off. When they arrived home the weary dog headed upstairs to his bed. A few minutes later Miss Linda was following behind with a bowl of food. As she entered the bedroom, she looked down at Boo's bed and saw that he was fast asleep. He was even snoring.

As she clicked out the light she spoke softly, "Boo...I don't know what I would do if I really lost you...after all you really *are* my little boy."

Draw a picture about this chapter or one of
Boo Boo on the boat

"Papa Boo"

Miss Linda's house wasn't the biggest one on the street, nor was it the smallest. It was an in-between size house with a small front porch and a big backyard. At the rear of the house was another porch where Boo Boo would sometimes sit for hours watching the birds, squirrels and chipmunks play in the garden.

Nothing really exciting went on in the backyard except for the time when Miss Linda and Boo Boo were stung by some angry bees. Things were pretty quiet in their yard...that's until something happened one day in April that they would never forget.

One morning Boo Boo was gazing out of an open window when he heard some strange noises. He had never heard anything like it before and wanted to investigate where the strange sounds were coming from.

He let out a quiet bark and Miss Linda opened the door for him. He ran out onto the porch and then down the steps in search of the strange sounds. It was then that he made a discovery. Under the porch, nestled in an old seed box, were three strange creatures. They glanced over at Boo Boo and said, "Meow!"

What's a "Meow?" Boo Boo wondered.

And what in the world were these strange furry animals doing under his porch?

He decided to show Miss Linda what he had found so he went to the back door and barked softly to get her attention.

"What's up Boo?" she called to him.

"Woof!" He replied and turned around hoping Miss Linda would follow him. And she did.

Boo Boo crawled under the porch and Miss Linda kneeled down and peered through an opening.

"My goodness…where did they come from?" she called to Boo Boo. He slowly moved closer to the seed box and began to growl.

"No, no, Boo, they're just kittens and they won't harm you."

Kittens? What are kittens? Boo Boo asked himself.

Miss Linda began to wonder what happened to their mother and why she had chosen their house to have her babies.

Boo Boo spent the entire day going in and out under the back porch. By late afternoon the kittens cried out with even louder, "meows!"

Miss Linda knew they had to take care of these visitors so she moved the box to the top of the porch.

In the late afternoon the kittens would not stop crying so she decided to try to feed them some milk using an eyedropper. Boo Boo also wanted to help too. He figured someone had to protect them when it got dark, so he decided to sleep with the three kittens that night. Miss Linda moved the babies inside the back porch door to keep them warm.

During the night when they cried, Boo Boo would lick their little faces. He really didn't like their scent, but he knew a little kiss now and then during the night would make them feel better.

When night ended and the morning sun came up, Miss Linda once again fed the little critters some warm milk. She gazed out into her backyard but there was no mother cat in sight. She looked down and smiled when she saw the kittens snuggling against her little boy. She laughed with pride.

She didn't know how long this would last and was surprised that three days later Boo Boo continued to love the little kittens. After five days, she gave up hoping the mother cat could appear.

One night while Miss Linda and Boo Boo sat on the back porch looking at their furry visitors, she gently patted her Little Boy Boo on his back and spoke.

"Well I never thought I'd ever see a day when you acted like a father to some strange cats!" Boo Boo sat still and listened. "I think these little felines will get along without you tonight."

In the morning Boo Boo did not hear the usual cries of hunger coming from the three kitties. He went out to see his little friends, but they were no longer in the seed box.

"They're gone, Boo," explained Miss Linda.

Boo Boo Baxter sniffed the box, walked around it and stared up at his master with a sad look on his face. He listened as Miss Linda spoke softly.

"Yes, Boo, they're gone...and you saved them. I gave them milk but you gave them the thing they needed most...love!"

Boo Boo still had a sad look on his face so Miss Linda bent down, raised his front paws and nuzzled her nose against his.

LOVE! Yes, love is the most important thing one creature can give to another. Boo Boo Baxter knew all about love because he was loved by the most wonderful creature in the whole wide world...Miss Linda.

Draw a picture about this chapter or one of
Boo Boo and the little kittens

"Broken Bone Boo"

Like other little boys, Boo Boo loved to run and play. Sometimes Miss Linda would look in the backyard and see him jumping up at a butterfly or chasing the big fat squirrel who liked to hide his acorns in the ground.

One day she watched him leap off the porch to try to catch that squirrel, but he was too quick and Boo Boo landed on a garden tool and hurt his belly. Miss Linda ran to check on him and when she saw that he could not move, gently lifted him into her arms.

She brought him to his bed where he barked a different kind of bark. "*I'm hurting*," is what he was trying to tell her. Miss Linda knew exactly what to do and called Dr. Rubenstein.

"Bring him right over to my office!" the doctor told her.

Twenty minutes later the injured dog lay on the doctor's examination table.

"Well, Mr. Baxter," (As you might remember, he always called him, Mr. Baxter) "this time you've really done it! I feel a broken bone and only an x-ray will let us know for sure if you've got one...or maybe two!" he finished.

As Boo Boo rested on the table, the doctor brought in his portable x-ray machine and took a picture. A few minutes later, after he had developed the negative he re-entered the examination room. As he held the x-ray film up to the light, Miss Linda gently petted her little boy. Sure enough, he had a fractured rib.

"Linda, there is really nothing we can do. Make him comfortable and allow his little body to heal itself. Of course you'll have to be very gentle with him. It will take time for the bone to mend, but I'm sure he'll make it through," Dr. Rubenstein explained as he looked into the little dog's face and smiled.

"Mr. Baxter, I'm going to give you some medicine for the pain." He gently placed a tasty pill on Boo Boo's tongue and he swallowed it in one gulp. Dr Rubinstein smiled because Boo Boo was such a good patient. He was the veterinarian for Boo Boo's father, *Baxter*, his mother, *Brittany* and all of his brothers and sisters too!

The doctor's nurses brought out a special carrier for Miss Linda to use to carry him home.

She drove the car very slowly and tried to avoid any bumps in the road. Boo Boo lay at her side.

When they arrived home she placed Boo Boo in his bed. He was still in so much pain that he couldn't fall asleep.

While he lay there Miss Linda looked down and remembered the wonderful day when Boo Boo Baxter first came into her life.

She had been thinking about getting a dog for a long time and finally one day she decided to go to the animal pound where dogs and cats were waiting to be adopted. By chance, in the parking lot she met a woman carrying a basket with a little Yorkshire terrier puppy in it.

"Oh, how cute he is!" Miss Linda remarked as she looked into the puppy's face and listened as the woman began to talk about him.

"I just can't seem to find a home for this one. His brothers and sisters flew out the door...I mean people came and took them right after they were weaned. This little guy didn't catch anyone's attention, so I'm bringing him here, hoping he'll be adopted. My husband

and I are moving to a smaller apartment and can't take him with us."

"He's so adorable!" Miss Linda whispered softly.

"Would you like to take him home?" the woman asked.

Miss Linda was stunned! What should she do? She did want a dog, but was she really ready to make a decision. She had told herself not to get too attached to the dogs or she might take all of them home. Taking care of a dog was a big responsibility.

"Why don't we go into the pound and you can play with him while I get him registered!" the woman suggested.

Miss Linda was relieved. She did want to see the other dogs before choosing one. A few minutes later she was holding the lady's little Yorkshire terrier puppy in her arms. He nuzzled his little nose into her coat and fell asleep. As he dozed, Miss Linda walked around and looked at all the other dogs. There were big dogs, little dogs, barking dogs and sleeping dogs. Some of the dogs were noisy and unfriendly. She continued to walk around when all of a sudden, the little pooch in her arms looked up and called to her with a gentle bark.

"Aren't you beautiful!" she exclaimed as she pulled him closer to her chest.

As she spoke, the man who worked at the pound walked over to the women and began to reach for the little dog in Miss Linda's arms.

"Well, I guess I'd better take this one and get him registered," he said to the ladies as he continued to reach for the puppy.

"I don't think you'll need to register this one. I'm going to take him to his new home on Pendale Street!"

Now, five years later, her little boy was in his cuddle bed with a broken bone.

She looked down at Boo Boo and saw that he was still in pain, so she gave him another pill and he began to fall asleep.

Oh, how she loved him!

She stroked his little paws and remembered the time he walked on the beach and got a little stone caught in one of them. She noticed that Boo Boo was limping and reached down to inspect his paws. She remembered how Boo Boo let her remove it. No matter what happened he always trusted his master to help him.

Miss Linda spent the evening remembering all the wonderful times she shared with her special dog. And when it was time for her to go to sleep, she placed Boo Boo's bed at the side of her own bed and lowered her hand to touch him. She would be there for him, no matter what happened. After all, Boo Boo Baxter *was* her little boy!

THE END

Draw a picture about this chapter or one of
Miss Linda holding Boo Boo

Hi Reader,

Now it's your turn to have fun!

On the next pages you'll find some puzzles, learning games and special lined pages for YOU to write your own chapter about Boo Boo Baxter and illustrate it too!

David Mercaldo, Author

Oh, by the way...
"The Further Adventures of Little Boy Boo"
...will be available soon!

Visit www.davidmercaldo.com for information.

HOW MANY WORDS CAN YOU MAKE FROM THE NAME

Boo Boo Baxter?

1. Boo Boo
2. Boob
3.
4.
5.
6.
7.
8.
9.
10.
11.
12.
13.
14.
15.

16.
17.
18.
19.
20.
21.
22.
23.
24.
25.
26.
27.
28.
29.
3O.

MAZE - Boo Boo is lost. Help him find his way home!

**Boo Boo starts
for home
here...**

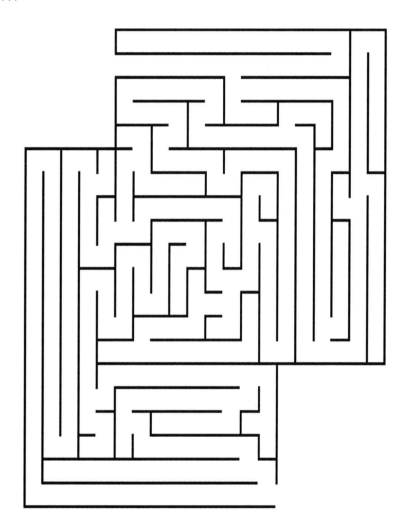

Pendale Street
"Home Sweet Home"

Crossword Puzzle

CROSSWORD PUZZLE CLUES

Across

3. The street where Boo Boo lives
4. The visitor who came after it snowed
6. A boy who learned to love Boo Boo
8. Boo Boo was lost on this
9. Kind of bear found under the park bench
10. Boo Boo's last name

Down

1. Highland terrier that lived on Oak St.
2. Miss Linda was stung by one of these
3. Where dogs and cats can be adopted
4. Pug who came on Thanksgiving
5. The state where Aunt Matilda lives
7. Boo Boo's master
10. The way a dog speaks
11. Color of Boo Boo's favorite sweater

WORD SEARCH *(level one)*

```
N  F  B  K  I  T  T  E  N  S
L  A  E  N  O  B  Y  O  O  B
B  I  M  B  T  Y  P  A  V  J
Y  E  N  W  O  J  U  A  L  Z
V  Z  E  D  O  A  M  D  R  P
D  R  A  Y  A  N  T  N  R  K
R  E  T  X  A  B  S  U  T  P
F  E  T  C  H  Y  O  O  E  A
X  R  A  Y  E  R  D  P  V  W
R  B  V  K  W  K  R  A  B  S
```

BARK	BAXTER	BEE	BOAT
BONE	BOO	FETCH	KEY
KITTENS	LINDA	PARK	PAWS
PLAY	POUND	SNOWMAN	VET
XRAY	YARD		

MATCHING GAME

Draw a line to match the items in the columns

Column A   **Column B**

Christie   The repairman

George   Miss Linda's friend
                                                from kindergarten

Karen   Randall's sister

Amy   Neighbor

Mr. Wilson   Lost her Teddy bear

Column A	Column B
"Boo Boo"	Boxer
"Mimi"	Highland terrier
"Frankie"	Yorkshire terrier
"Max"	Pug
"Simon"	French poodle

Write your own adventure about Boo Boo Baxter
on these pages

Chapter title _____

Written By _____

_____

_____

_____

_____

_____

_____

_____

_____

_____

_____

_____

_____

_____

_____

_____

Draw a picture here to illustrate your story

Breinigsville, PA USA
19 January 2011
253654BV00002B/269-1400/P

9 781615 790999